Evangeline

for Young Readers

Story by Hélène Boudreau
Illustrations by Patsy MacKinnon

NIMBUS
PUBLISHING

for Mémé — H. B.
for Angela, model extraordinaire. — P. M.

Nimbus Publishing Limited
3731 Mackintosh St, Halifax, NS B3K 5A5
(902) 455-4286 nimbus.ca

Printed and bound in Canada

Author photo: Natasha Boudreau
Illustrator photo: Philip Durand
Design: Heather Bryan
NB1001

Library and Archives Canada Cataloguing in Publication

Boudreau, Hélène, 1969-
Evangeline for young readers / Hélène Boudreau ;
illustrations by Patsy MacKinnon.

Prose adaptation of Henry Wadsworth Longfellow's poem Evangeline.
Issued also in electronic format.
ISBN 978-1-77108-010-1

I. MacAulay-MacKinnon, Patsy, 1952- II. Longfellow, Henry Wadsworth, 1807-1882. Evangeline. III. Title.

PS8603.O9267E83 2013   jC813'.6   C2012-907376-8

Nimbus Publishing acknowledges the financial support for its publishing activities from the Government of Canada through the Canada Book Fund (CBF) and the Canada Council for the Arts, and from the Province of Nova Scotia through the Department of Communities, Culture and Heritage.

Chapter One

❖

Long ago, in the land of Acadie, there lived a young woman named Evangeline Bellefontaine. Evangeline was the star in her father's eyes and was admired by many young men.

Evangeline's small Acadian village of Grand Pré sat on the shores of the Minas Basin. Villagers grew flax and corn and hay for their animals in vast meadows by the sea.

The children of Grand Pré played in the roads in front of simple houses. Women spun flax, milked cows, and ran the households. The men worked long days, farming the fields. The Acadians lived simply and in peace.

Evangeline's father, Benedict Bellefontaine, was a well-respected farmer. Her mother was no longer alive, but

Evangeline held her memory dear. She wore her mother's earrings brought over from their old country of France.

The Bellefontaine house stood on a hill by the sea a little apart from the village. There was an orchard nearby and barns for the horses and sheep. A proud turkey strutted around the farmyard and a noisy cock marked the hours of the day.

Many young men came to Evangeline's door, hoping to win her love. But Evangeline's heart belonged to one person: Gabriel Lajeunesse. Gabriel was the son of Basil the blacksmith. The blacksmith was an honoured role in the village, and Basil was Benedict the farmer's friend.

Evangeline and Gabriel grew up together. They learned their letters by studying church hymns with Father Felician.

After lessons, they would rush to the blacksmith's door to watch Basil work. They played in Benedict the farmer's barn and ran through the meadows and along the hillside. Their childhood was simple and carefree.

But time passed, and soon Evangeline and Gabriel were not children anymore.

Chapter Two

Years went by and seasons changed. One fall, the bees hoarded extra honey in their hives and the fox's coat was thicker than usual. The Mi'kmaq hunters predicted a long, cold winter.

Benedict the farmer stayed warm by a large fire after a hard day's work in the fields. He sang old French songs while Evangeline sat at his side, spinning flax for the loom.

As they sat, the door swung open. It was Basil the blacksmith and, to Evangeline's delight, his son Gabriel.

"Welcome, Basil, my friend," exclaimed Benedict the farmer happily. "Come sit close to the fire."

"Benedict Bellefontaine. You are always so cheerful even when others are filled with gloom," replied Basil the

blacksmith as he joined his friend by the fireside. "English ships have been anchored in our harbour for four days now. They have their cannons pointed toward us. Tomorrow the men of our village are to meet at the church to hear a message from King George. It is to become the law of the land."

Benedict the farmer was thoughtful for a moment. "Maybe they come for a friendly purpose. Perhaps England's harvests have not been good. They may need some of our fine crops."

"That is not what the villagers think. Many have already fled into the forest." Basil the blacksmith heaved a sigh. "The English have taken away our weapons. How are we supposed to defend ourselves if it comes to that?"

"We are farmers, not fighters. We're better off unarmed, amid our fields and flocks," Benedict the farmer said. "But let us not think of it tonight. This is a happy day!"

Benedict motioned to Evangeline, who stood by the window hand in hand with Gabriel. "This is the night of our children's contract to be married. René Leblanc will be here soon with his ink and papers to make it official."

Evangeline blushed at her father's words. As she did, René the notary entered through the door.

Chapter Three

"Have you heard more news from the villagers?" Basil the blacksmith asked René the notary as he entered the Bellefontaine home. "What do they think of the English ships in our harbour?"

"I have heard gossip, but we are at peace, not war," René replied as he shook Basil's hand. "Why would the English harm us?"

"They have guns and powder!" exclaimed Basil the blacksmith. "We have nothing. They can do whatever they like!"

René the notary had twenty children and was loved by all. He had lived many years and seen many things.

"Man may not be fair, but God is fair," answered the notary thoughtfully. And then he told the story of a statue that stood in the middle of a city in an ancient land. The statue was a symbol of justice. Birds nested within a set of scales held in the statue's left hand.

Over time, the land became corrupted. One day an orphan girl was accused of stealing a strand of pearls from a nobleman. She faced her sentence at the feet of the statue.

Suddenly, a tremendous bolt of lightning exploded from the heavens. It hit the statue and the scales fell to the ground along with the bird's nest. Within the nest was the missing strand of pearls. The girl was set free.

"Justice will triumph," finished René the notary.

Basil the blacksmith listened quietly, but his face was still creased with worry.

Evangeline lit the lamp on the table. She filled a tankard with strong brew as René the notary wrote out the papers for her marriage to Gabriel. Once everything was in order, her father, Benedict the farmer, paid René three times his normal fee with solid pieces of silver.

The bride and groom to be were toasted with ale and blessed by the notary. Later, Evangeline crept up to her room. She folded the linens and woollen things she'd made for her marriage. Her heart was filled with hope but also sadness.

She thought of René the notary's story but also of Basil the blacksmith's concern.

What fate awaited the people of Acadie?

Chapter Four

The next day the Acadian men of Grand Pré were called to the church.

"You are brought here today by His Majesty's orders." The English commander spoke to the men from the church's altar. "It is his will that your lands, houses, and animals become property of the English Crown. You will be deported from this province and transported to other lands."

At first the Acadian men were stunned and silent, but they soon realized the meaning of the commander's words. They rushed for the church's doors to escape but the English soldiers blocked their way. Basil the blacksmith raised his arms and shouted wildly.

"Tyrants! Death to these foreign soldiers who seize our homes and our harvests!" But before he could say more, Basil the blacksmith was struck to the ground by one of the soldiers.

"What has come over you?" Father Felician entered his church and addressed the Acadians. "For forty years I've tried to teach you to love one another. Have you forgotten God's lessons of love and forgiveness? Oh Father, forgive them!"

The Acadian men fell to their knees and repeated Father Felician's prayer.

Meanwhile, Evangeline waited at home with the table set for dinner, but Gabriel and her father never arrived. She wandered to the village and lingered in the churchyard with the other women of the village, looking for Gabriel.

"Gabriel!" she cried. But there was no answer. Soon, news of the Deportation spread amongst the women, filling Evangeline's heart with dread.

How can this be happening? Evangeline wondered. She tried to remember René the notary's story of the pearls in the bird's nest. Surely, justice would triumph and the men of Grand Pré would be returning to their homes before long!

Chapter Five

Five days later, the Acadian women and children of Grand Pré were ordered to board the English ships waiting in the harbour. They travelled from the countryside with carts and oxen and piled their belongings along the shore. Evangeline waited for her father and Gabriel by her trunk filled with dowry linens and possessions.

Finally, Evangeline spotted Gabriel as the men of the village were led to the shore from the church. They sang as they marched. *"Fill our hearts this day with strength…"*

"Gabriel!" Evangeline ran to him and clasped his hand. "Be of good cheer! If we love one another, nothing, in truth, can harm us."

But then Evangeline noticed her father in the group. Being held prisoner in the church had been difficult for him. His face was pale and his footsteps heavy. Evangeline rushed to his side.

Long rowboats transported the Acadian villagers to the waiting ships. Amid the confusion, wives became separated from their husbands. Children were left behind on land. To Evangeline's horror, Gabriel and Basil the blacksmith were forced onto a waiting ship while she was left on shore with her father.

Night fell and Benedict the farmer got weaker. Father Felician came to Evangeline's side and offered words of comfort.

"Benedict," murmured Father Felician. But the old farmer was too weak to answer. The priest and Evangeline sat silently by his side.

Suddenly, the darkened sky lit up as the houses of the village were set on fire.

"We shall never again see our homes in the village of Grand Pré," cried the crowd.

Evangeline stood in shock, overwhelmed that the English soldiers had burned her village to the ground. She turned to her father. But Benedict the farmer had fallen to the ground and died.

Evangeline knelt beside her father and wept. All night she lay beside him, and when morning came the rowboats restarted their journeys to the waiting English ships.

"Let us bury him here by the sea," Father Felician suggested.

Evangeline sailed away from her home of Grand Pré with her father buried on the shore, Gabriel on another ship, and her village in ruins.

Chapter Six

Many years passed since the Deportation from Grand Pré. The Acadians were forced to make new lives in faraway cities and towns. Some were returned to France. Others were scattered throughout the New World, from the cold lakes of the North to the hot savannahs of the South. Many drowned or died along the way and never made it to their destination.

Evangeline travelled from place to place with Father Felician, searching for Gabriel.

Sometimes she spoke with someone who knew him.

"Gabriel Lajeunesse!" they said. "Oh, yes! We have seen him. He was with Basil the blacksmith, and both have gone to the prairies. They are *coureurs des bois*, and famous hunters and trappers."

"Gabriel Lajeunesse!" said others. "Oh, yes! We have seen him. He is a *voyageur* in the lowlands of Louisiana."

But others discouraged Evangeline from her long, hard journey to search for Gabriel.

"Dear child!" they said. "Why dream and wait for him longer? Are there no other youths as fair as Gabriel? Here is Baptiste Leblanc, the notary's son. He has loved you for many years. Come, give him your hand and be happy!"

"I cannot!" Evangeline replied sadly. "Where my heart has gone, my hand follows, and not elsewhere. My heart lights the way, making everything clear. Everything else lies in darkness."

Father Felician had travelled many miles with Evangeline and understood her troubles.

"Love is never wasted," Father Felician said with a smile. "And patience will help you accomplish your labour of love."

Evangeline kept on her journey to find Gabriel, encouraged by Father Felician's words. But as she travelled, at times she couldn't help wandering through village graveyards, her eyes scanning the tombstones for Gabriel's name.

Chapter Seven

One May, Evangeline and Father Felician sailed along the Mississippi River. Their boat was filled with men, women, and children searching for their long-lost families from Acadie.

Evangeline imagined that every stroke of the boatmen's oars brought her nearer and nearer to Gabriel.

Day after day, they sailed southward along the turbulent river. Night after night, they camped on the riverbanks. The weather became warmer as they travelled further south. Soon, the Acadian boatmen arrived in the confusing watery maze of the bayou, and eventually stopped to rest beside a group of islands covered with trees.

A swifter boat travelled northward through the bayou among the many islands. This other boat was filled with hunters and trappers on their way to the land of bison and beaver.

Gabriel sat at this boat's helm. After years of waiting for Evangeline, he'd grown unhappy and restless. He thought the adventures of the Wild West would help him get over his sorrow.

Gabriel's boat took no notice of Evangeline's boat hidden under the trees on the other side of the islands. Swiftly, the hunters and trappers glided away as the Acadians slept.

"Oh, Father Felician!" Evangeline awoke with a start. "Something says in my heart that Gabriel wanders near me."

"Gabriel is truly near thee," Father Felician replied. "Not far away to the south of us is the Eden of Louisiana. Our Acadian brothers and sisters are there, waiting for us. There, you can reunite with your long-lost love."

With these words, the Acadians arose and continued on their journey. They rowed onward, through the still waters, under the overhanging branches of willows.

Finally, they arrived to the promised land of Louisiana. Off in the distance, they were welcomed by the horn of a herdsman and the sound of lowing cattle.

Chapter Eight

The sturdy house of a herdsman stood near the bank of the river. A thin blue column of smoke from the chimney greeted the weary Acadian travellers.

The herdsman returned from his flock on the prairie. He rode his horse up the path to the garden behind his house, mounted on his Spanish saddle. It was Gabriel's father, Basil the blacksmith.

Basil gazed from under his wide sombrero at the familiar faces of Father Felician and Evangeline. He dismounted from his horse and greeted them with laughter and friendly embraces.

"How did you miss my Gabriel's boat in the bayous?" Basil asked.

"Is Gabriel gone?" Tears filled Evangeline's eyes.

"Be of good cheer," Basil the blacksmith replied. "He is not far on his way. Up and away tomorrow, we will follow him fast and bring him back."

Others arrived at Basil's doorstep from nearby homesteads. Happy voices filled the air as the Acadian travellers met their old friends and family with hugs and tears.

"Welcome once more, my friends," Basil the blacksmith announced, "who so long have been friendless and homeless. Welcome once more to a home, that is better perchance than the old one! No King George of England shall drive you away from your homesteads, burning your dwellings and barns, and stealing your farms and your cattle."

Michael the fiddler's music filled the air. The travellers danced and drank the night away, relieved to finally be reunited with their old friends from Acadie.

Meanwhile, Evangeline stood nearby, as if in a daze. She remembered another time when Michael the fiddler played such music—on the day she and Gabriel celebrated their engagement.

"Oh, Gabriel!" Evangeline cried as she wandered through the garden in the moonlight. "How often have you walked this path to the prairie? How often have you looked on the woodlands around me? How often, under this oak, have you rested after a long day's work and dreamt of me? When will I see and hold you again?"

"Patience," the oak tree seemed to whisper.

"Tomorrow," the meadow answered.

The next morning, Father Felician bid Evangeline and Basil the blacksmith goodbye. "Farewell! Bring us Gabriel from his adventures.

"Farewell!" answered Evangeline as she boarded the boat.

They followed Gabriel's journey, guided by rumours of his whereabouts. They did not find him the first day, or the next, or for many days afterward. Finally, Evangeline and Basil the blacksmith arrived at an inn and spoke to the landlord.

There they learned that Gabriel had been at the inn the day before but had left the village and taken the road to the prairies.

Chapter Nine

Far into the western country, the land was untamed and dangerous. Herds of buffalo, elk, and wild horses roamed over miles and miles of grassy prairies. Wolves and bears hunted through deep valleys running between snow-capped mountains.

Gabriel had travelled deep into this wilderness with other hunters and trappers. Day after day, Evangeline and Basil the blacksmith searched for him with the help of their Native American guides. Sometimes they thought they saw the smoke from his campfire off in the distance. Once they got there, though, all they found were ashes.

One night, a Shawnee woman wandered into Evangeline and Basil's camp. She was travelling back to her people because her Canadian husband, a *coureur des bois*, had been murdered.

Evangeline listened to her sad tale of lost love. She wept at the Shawnee woman's words and told her own story of her search for Gabriel. A thoughtful look crossed the Shawnee woman's face before she spoke.

"The fair Lilinau was once wooed by a phantom," the Shawnee woman began. "The phantom breathed love through the pines over Lilinau's father's lodge. Lilinau followed the phantom's whispers through the forest. She was never seen again by her people."

Evangeline wondered if she was like the woman in the story, Lilinau. Was she chasing a phantom through the woods, too? Would she ever find Gabriel or was she cursed to wander looking for him forever?

The next morning, Evangeline and Basil the blacksmith got ready to continue their journey.

"Go to the mission on the western slope of these mountains," the Shawnee woman suggested. "There, the Black Robe chief teaches the people about Mary and Jesus. It fills their hearts with joy to hear him."

"Let us go to the mission," Evangeline decided. "Good tidings await us."

Once they arrived, Evangeline was relieved to hear the familiar sounds of her mother tongue. They were greeted warmly by the priest and led into his wigwam to rest. To Evangeline's surprise, the priest had news of Gabriel.

"Gabriel sat on the mat where you rest just six days ago," the priest said. "He told me the same sad tale as you, then

continued on his journey. He has gone to hunt but will return in autumn."

"Let me stay with you and wait," Evangeline said, tired and sad from the many disappointments of her journey. Basil the blacksmith returned to his homestead and Evangeline stayed at the mission.

Days and weeks and months passed, but Gabriel did not return. Autumn came, then winter and spring, and still nothing.

Finally, news came in the summer that Gabriel had a lodge by the banks of the Saginaw River. Saying a sad farewell, Evangeline left the mission to find him. But after a long and dangerous journey, all she discovered was a deserted hunter's lodge.

For years after, Evangeline wandered from missions to battlefields to towns and cities, travelling like a phantom. She had started her journey young and full of hope.

But as the years passed and she grew older, her hope of ever finding Gabriel slowly faded away.

Chapter Ten

Finally, after many years of roaming without finding Gabriel, Evangeline settled by the Delaware River. The Quaker people there reminded her of her old Acadian village of Grand Pré. She had finally found a home in exile.

In Evangeline's memory, Gabriel was still the young man she'd once loved. But in her heart, it was like he had passed away, not been lost. With all hope of ever finding Gabriel gone, Evangeline dedicated her life as a Sister of Mercy and tended to the sick and poor.

Over time, disease fell on the city. One morning Evangeline entered the almshouse where the poorest of the sick were sent to die. Something inside her said, "At last, your trials have ended."

Evangeline entered the chamber of sickness, offering help to those who lay dying. Many had passed away through the night. Many others had taken their places.

Suddenly, a shudder ran through Evangeline. An old man lay on the bed before her. He was long and thin with graying hair, but his face remained the same.

It was Gabriel, now old and dying of sickness.

"Gabriel! Oh, my beloved!" Evangeline whispered.

Gabriel heard her voice through his fever and dreamed of the home of his childhood in Grand Pré. He thought of his long-lost green Acadian meadows, rivers, mountains and woodlands, and, of course, of Evangeline. When he opened his eyes, Evangeline was there, kneeling by his bedside.

Gabriel tried to whisper her name, but no sound came out. He tried to sit up, but his body was too weak. Soon, the light faded from his eyes and Evangeline kissed his dying lips.

It was over now. Evangeline could feel all the hope, the fear, the sorrow and pain leave her body as Gabriel passed away. She pressed his lifeless body to her chest one last time and bowed her head.

"Thank you, God," Evangeline prayed.

Side by side in nameless graves, Evangeline and Gabriel are sleeping.

In the middle of the city where they lie, they go unknown and unnoticed.

Many miles and lifetimes away, their childhood home of Grand Pré remains. Some Acadians returned from exile to

live there again. Others with new customs and languages have made their homes there in the shade of the forest by the sea.

And still, over the whirr of the loom by the evening fire, they repeat Evangeline and Gabriel's tale of undying love while the sea and the forest echo with the sounds of Acadie.

The Acadians

In the seventeenth century, French settlers began arriving in what we call North America. Their descendants in Canada's Maritime Provinces as well as parts of what are now New England and Maine came to be called Acadians. Most of the Acadians lived by the Bay of Fundy in Nova Scotia. They built dikes holding back the tides along the coastline to create lush farmland, and lived peacefully with each other and with the Mi'kmaq.

However, the peace did not last very long. The British and French governments were fighting over the land the Acadians lived on. Britain took control of the area in 1710, and for the next forty-five years they tried to make the

Acadians sign an oath of allegiance, saying that they were loyal to the British king. The Acadians would not sign the oath, for a number of reasons.

In 1755, the British government decided they did not want people who may not be loyal to the British Empire living in a place that the British were still fighting over, and they deported about 11,500 Acadians (around 75 percent of them) over the next seven years. All of their lands and belongings were taken from them, and they were sent in ships to other British colonies and, in some cases, back to France.

Even though their communities were broken up and some families were separated, the Acadians managed to continue their cultural traditions. Many went to Louisiana, and they began to be called Cajuns. Others returned to the British settlements they had been expelled from, though many of their lands had already been claimed by new settlers.

Today, there are Acadians all over the world, but they still live mostly in the Maritime provinces, as well as in parts of Quebec, Maine, and Louisiana. Since 1994, Acadians from all over the world have gathered every five years to celebrate their culture and history together, at a festival called the *Congrès mondial acadien*, or the World Acadian Congress. The Acadian culture is as vibrant as ever, and continues on in contemporary writing, music, plays, and art.

Henry Wadsworth Longfellow
and *Evangeline*

Henry Wadsworth Longfellow was an American poet. Born in 1807 in Maine, he published his first poem in a newspaper when he was thirteen years old. He worked as a professor of languages after graduating school, and continued to write and publish poems as well.

In 1847, Longfellow published his poem *Evangeline*, a long narrative poem telling a fictionalized account of the Acadian Deportation. It was Longfellow's most popular poem when he was alive, and is still one of his best-known works. Readers were drawn to the tragic story of Evangeline and Gabriel, and the poem generated interest in the Deportation. Many believe that *Evangeline* helped the Acadian people revive their culture.

Evangeline has inspired many other creative works, including music, plays, and film—in 1913, *Evangeline* was adapted into a movie, becoming the first Canadian feature-length film.

There is a statue of Evangeline, erected in 1920, at the Grand Pré National Historic Site. It is outside the reconstructed church there, and both are visited by thousands of people every year.

Longfellow died in 1882, but his poetry, especially his heartbreaking portrayal of the Acadian Deportation, lives on.

Hélène Boudreau is an Acadian Métis author and artist. She grew up in the Acadian village of Petit de Grat, Nova Scotia, and now makes her home in Markham, Ontario. Her first middle grade novel, *Acadian Star*, was shortlisted for the 2009–2010 Hackmatack Children's Choice Book Award. Since then, Hélène has gone on to publish over a dozen fiction and non-fiction books for young people. You can visit her at www.heleneboudreau.com.

Patsy MacKinnon is the illustrator of *A Day with You in Paradise*, *Heartsong*, and *The Voyage of Wood Duck*. A member of the prestigious Canadian Society of Painters in Water Colour, Patsy lives in New Waterford, Nova Scotia.